This book belongs to

_____.

This book was read by

_____

on

_____.

Are you ready to start reading the **StoryPlay** way?

Read the story on its own. Play the activities together
as you read!

Ready. Set. Smart!

la-la!

by Karen Beaumont

illustrated by LeUyen Pham

Cartwheel Books
An Imprint of Scholastic Inc.

Text copyright © 2011 by Karen Beaumont
Illustrations copyright © 2011 by LeUyen Pham
Prompts and activities © 2017 by Scholastic Inc.

Library of Congress Cataloging-in-Publication Data available

ISBN 978-1-338-11555-0
10 9 8 7 6 5 4 3 2 1   17 18 19 20 21
Printed in Panyu, China   137
This edition first printing, January 2017
Book design by Doan Buu

For my daughters, Christina and Nicolyn.
I love you with all of my heart . . . and "sole"!
—K.B.

To Kay, the ultimate Shoe-Gal.
—L.P.

Party dresses, party hair . . .
Need new party shoes to wear.
Emily, Ashley, Kaitlyn, Claire!
Let's go find the perfect pair!

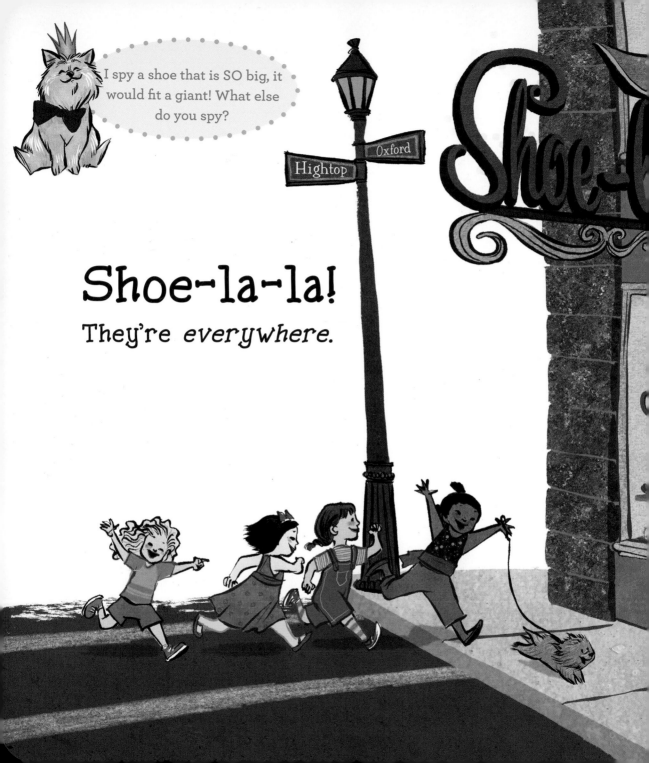

Rows and rows!
These or those?
Up, up on our tippy toes.
Can't wait to choose new shoes.
Here goes!

Who is your favorite person to go shopping with? Why?

Shoes with zippers,

Shoes with straps,

Shoes with buckles,

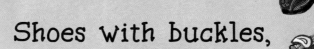

Shoes with taps.

Shoes with laces, shoes with bows,

Sorry, sir. We *don't* like those.
They hurt our toes.

I'll try on this rainbow pair.

Hey! These match my underwear!

I'm barking at the shoe with leopard spots on it. Can you guess why?

Lots and lots of leopard spots.

Pink and purple polka dots.

These show off
my pretty feet.

These look good
enough to eat.

Fuzzy boots for
when it snows.

Ballerina
on my toes!

Cowgirl . . .

Rock star . . .

Princess . . .

Bride . . .

This pair? That pair? Can't decide.

Fancy ribbons,
   Frilly lace.
Shoe-la-la!
   We *love* this place!

Describe your favorite pair of shoes! What can you do in them?

Sparkly diamonds, pretty pearls,
Ritzy, glitzy

Emily,
Ashley,
Kaitlyn,
Claire!
Hurry, hurry!
Pick a pair!

Piles and piles
fill the aisles.

Never seen
so many styles.

Do you see MORE than or
FEWER than 20 shoes?
How many can you count?

Shop and shop until we drop!
Guess it's time for us to STOP!

Eeny, meeny, my oh my!
Just don't know which shoes to buy.

Can't decide. We've seen too many.

Can you think of any words
that rhyme with *SHOE*?

Sorry, sir.
We *don't* want ANY!

Tried on every single shoe.
Don't know what we're going to do.

Can you guess what the girls are doing?

Party dresses,

Party hair . . .

Perfect party shoes to wear!

Can you think of something old that you would like to re-create? How would you do it?

Story time fun never ends with these creative activities!

★ When I Grow Up... ★

When the friends are trying on shoes, they imagine themselves as cowgirls, rock stars, and more! Have some fun imagining what you could be when you grow up!

When I grow up, I want to be a . . .
I will love it because . . .
I think the best part will be . . .

★ Draw Your Own Friend Adventure ★

Friends Emily, Ashley, Kaitlyn, and Claire go on a shoe-shopping adventure together! Can you think of an adventure you'd like to go on with your friends? Who would you invite on your adventure? Where would you go? Draw your own adventure story and then share it with your friends!